D0603245

BIG IDEA BOOKS

www.bigidea.com

Zonder**kidz**®

The children's group of Zondervan
www.zonderkidz.com

An Easter Carol
Copyright © 2004 by Big Idea Productions, Inc.
Illustrations copyright © 2004 by Big Idea Productions, Inc.

Requests for information should be addressed to:
Zonderkidz, Grand Rapids, Michigan 49530

All Scripture quotations, unless otherwise indicated, are taken from the
HOLY BIBLE, NEW INTERNATIONAL READER'S VERSION ®.
Copyright © 1995, 1996, 1998 by International Bible Society. Used by
permission of Zondervan. All Rights Reserved.

ISBN: 0-310-70673-4

All rights reserved. No part of this publication may be reproduced,
stored in a retrieval system, or transmitted in any form or by any
means—electronic, mechanical, photocopy, recording, or any other—
except for brief quotations in printed reviews, without the prior permission of the publisher.

Big Idea is a registered trademark of Big Idea Productions, Inc.

Zonderkidz is a trademark of Zondervan.

Editor: Phil Vischer
Art Direction and Design: Karen Poth
Written by: Cindy Kenney
Illustrated by: Greg Hardin and Robert Vann

Printed in China
04 05 06 07/HK/4 3 2 1

AN EASTER CAROL

Written by Cindy Kenney
Illustrated by Greg Hardin and Robert Vann

Based on the video story by John Duckworth
Written by Tim Hodge, Phil Vischer, and Keith Lango

BIG IDEA
BOOKS®

Zonderkidz

The snow had melted. Flowers were blooming. Spring was in the air! The townsfolk were busy getting ready for a special Easter service at St. Bart's Church.

Edmund tried to balance on his crutch. He steadied a box of letters and passed an 'O' to his dad. Edmund and his dad, Reverend Gilbert, were putting up a sign to tell everyone about a beautiful new, stained-glass window at the church.

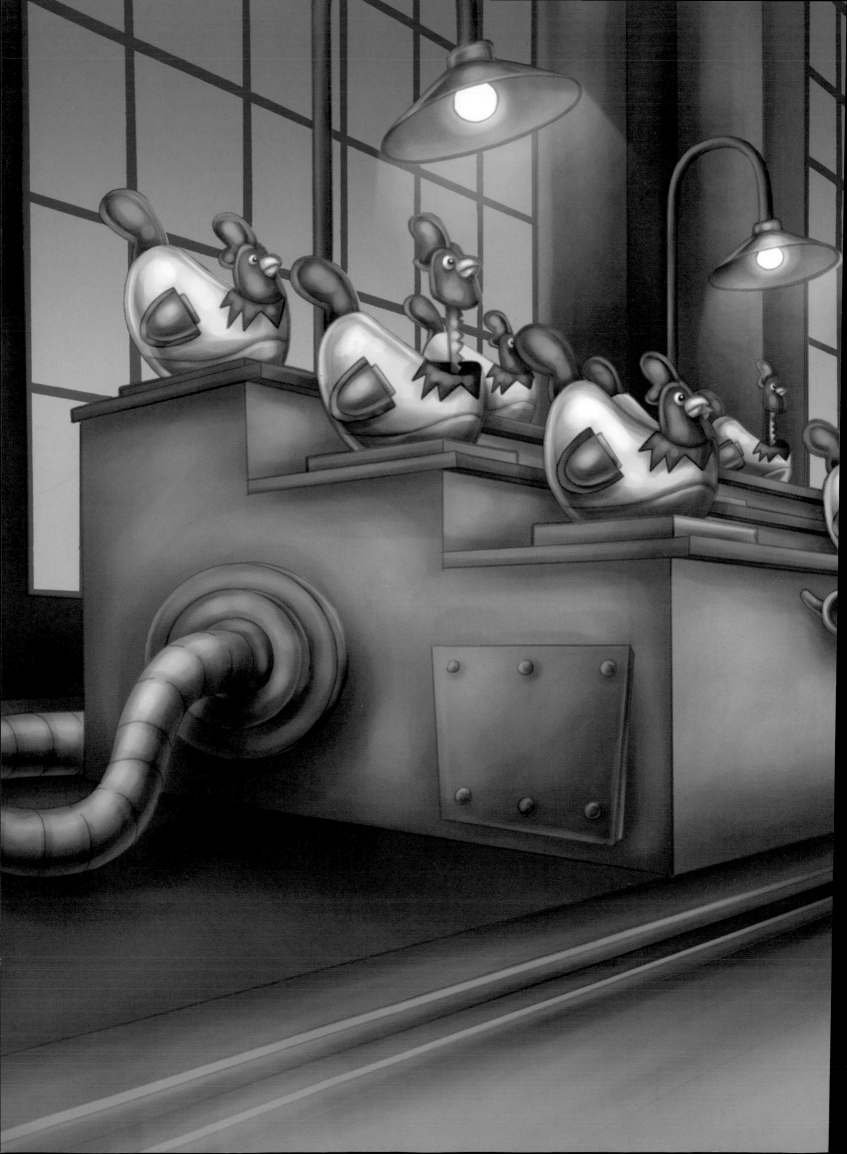

But not everyone cared about seeing the church window. Ebenezer Nezzer
was hard at work making Easter eggs in his factory.

All he cared about were the rows of mechanical chickens that laid colorful,
plastic eggs.

"Ah … the satisfying fatigue of productivity," Ebenezer giggled.

Ebenezer was unhappy when his work was interrupted by unexpected visitors.

"Mr. Nezzer, things are going so well in the factory," Cavis began. "Couldn't we close up shop just for Easter?"

"Remember how Grandmother Nezzer always brought you to church on Easter Sunday?" Reverend Gilbert added.

"Bah!" Ebenezer grumbled. "People are wasting their time sitting in those pews when they could be out buying more eggs! Instead of going to church, I'm going to build a place called Easter Land! Then everyone will buy my colored eggs and chocolate bunnies, and we can have Easter egg hunts every day."

"Look! I'll put Easter Land right *here*!" Ebenezer beamed as he plopped down a model of Easter Land right on top of St. Bart's Church. "Don't you just love it?"

"Y-y-you can't tear down the church!" cried Millward as the little steeple got crunched.

"Of course I can. This land has been in my family for generations. We're going to begin building tomorrow morning at eight o'clock!"

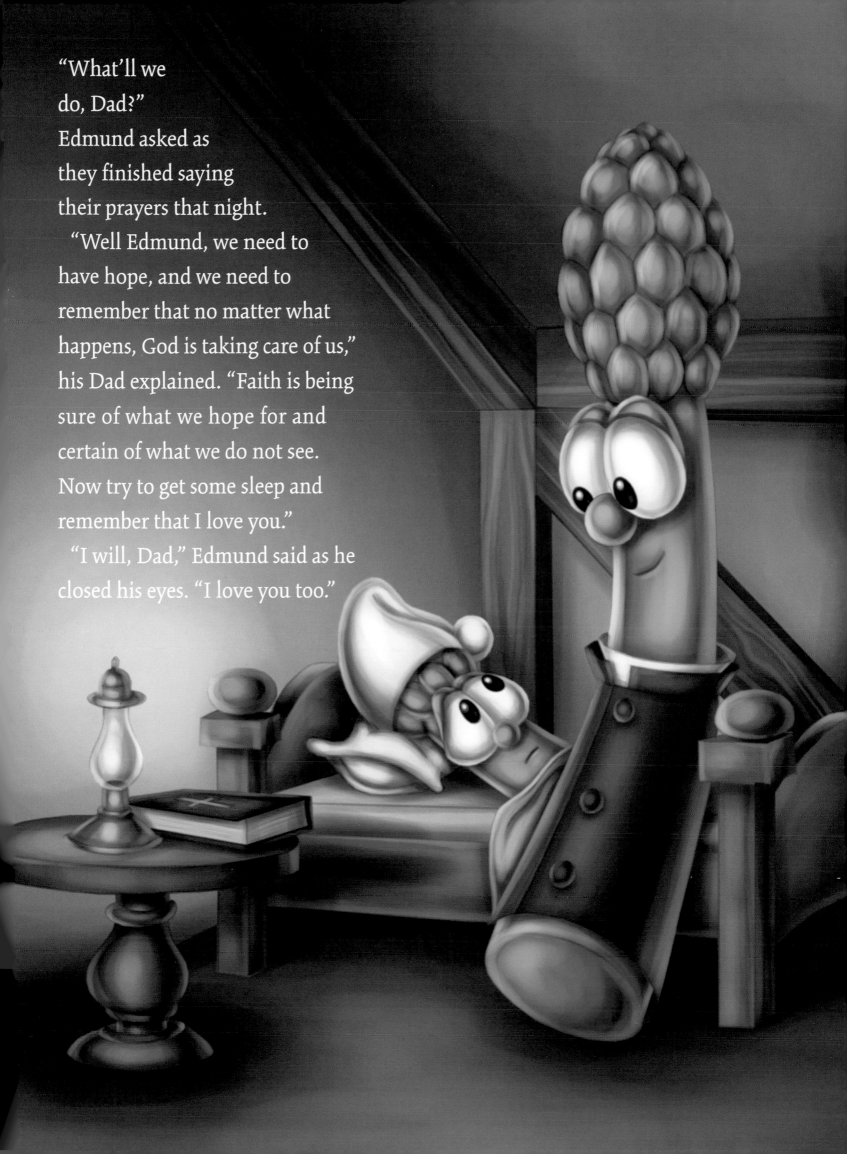

"What'll we do, Dad?" Edmund asked as they finished saying their prayers that night.

"Well Edmund, we need to have hope, and we need to remember that no matter what happens, God is taking care of us," his Dad explained. "Faith is being sure of what we hope for and certain of what we do not see. Now try to get some sleep and remember that I love you."

"I will, Dad," Edmund said as he closed his eyes. "I love you too."

That night, Ebenezer fell asleep right on his plans for Easter Land. And just as he began to snore, he was suddenly startled by his grandmother's voice!

"Ebenezer! Wake up!"

"Huh? Who's there?" Ebenezer asked. He was a little scared.

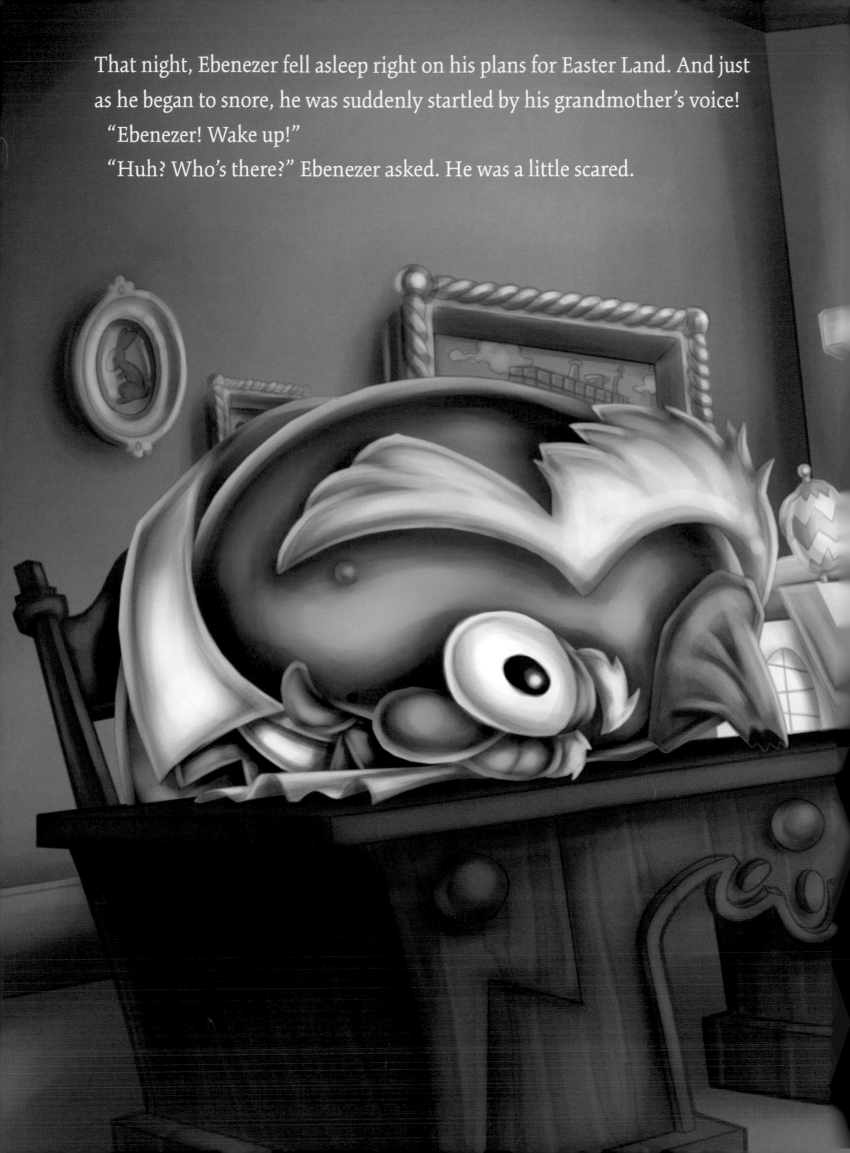

"It's me, your grandmother. You're having a vision. That's like a dream—with a point. And you missed it! You have Easter all backward and upside down. To help you figure it out, you will receive another visitor—at midnight!"

Then poof! Just like that—she was gone!

Outside, Cavis and Millward were trying to climb over the gate of Ebenezer's factory.

"Why do we want to break into the factory?" Millward asked.

"We have to get the plans. No plans—no Easter Land!" Cavis explained.

"It's just that the last time we borrowed something, it didn't go so well," Millward groaned.

Inside the factory, the clock moved toward midnight as Ebenezer once again fell asleep. When the clock struck twelve, an egg-shaped music box angel came to life and tapped Ebenezer on the head.

"Hey!" Ebenezer shouted as he tried to figure out who had hit him. "You're—you're—"

"My name is Hope, and I'm your worst nightmare!" the music-box angel chuckled as she flitted above his head.

Then she grabbed Ebenezer and out the window they flew!

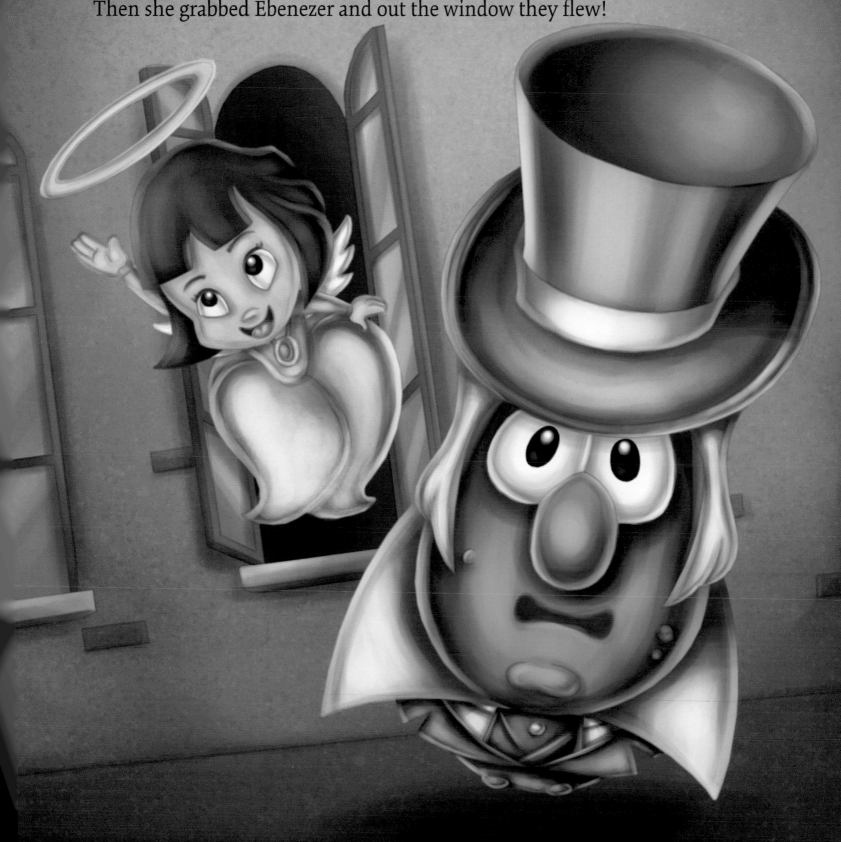

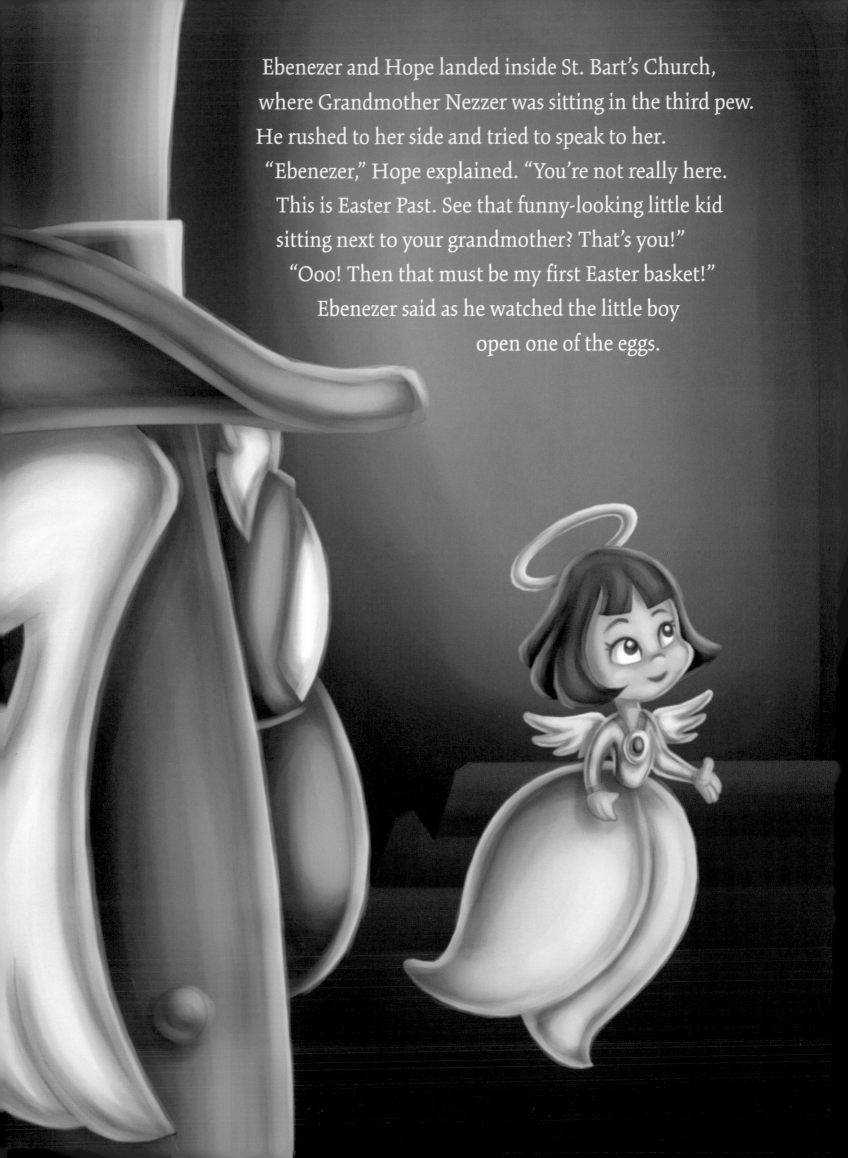

Ebenezer and Hope landed inside St. Bart's Church,
where Grandmother Nezzer was sitting in the third pew.
He rushed to her side and tried to speak to her.
"Ebenezer," Hope explained. "You're not really here.
This is Easter Past. See that funny-looking little kid
sitting next to your grandmother? That's you!"
"Ooo! Then that must be my first Easter basket!"
Ebenezer said as he watched the little boy
open one of the eggs.

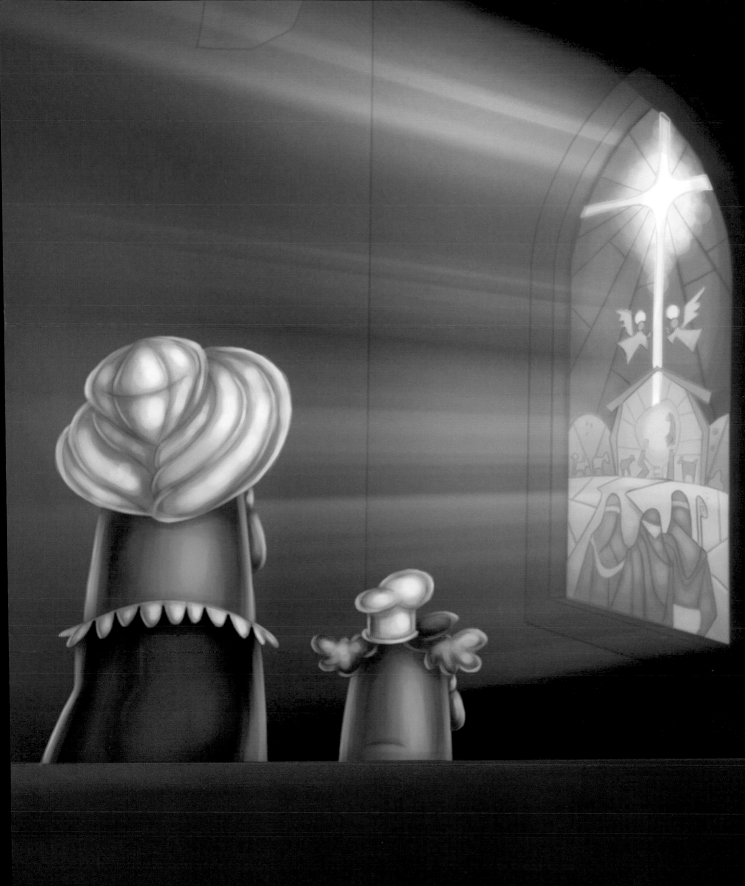

"It's empty," the little boy whispered.

"Yes, just like the tomb in the Easter story," his grandmother explained.

At that very moment, sunlight poured through a beautiful stained-glass window that showed the birth of Jesus.

"That's a really pretty picture," Ebenezer said, "but I don't understand."

With that, Hope pulled him away, and they flew right back to the factory.

This time Ebenezer saw himself all grown up.

"You called for an inventor?" asked Seymour Schwenk as he walked into the room.

"Yes, I did! I want to make Easter eggs around the clock! Can you make me some mechanical chickens that lay plastic eggs?"

"Sure—but Easter's not about plastic eggs," Seymour tried to tell him. But Ebenezer wouldn't listen.

In a split second, Ebenezer found himself standing outside the home of little Edmund Gilbert.

"This is Easter Present," Hope said.

"A present?" Ebenezer asked. "For me? Aww … you shouldn't have."

"No, not *a* present, *the* present. The here and now," Hope said, a little frustrated. But Ebenezer just didn't get it. So Hope gave him a nudge, and together they looked through Edmund's window.

"Mr. Nezzer just doesn't understand about Easter," Edmund said, as he began to cough. "He's not a bad man. He just doesn't have what we have. He doesn't have the hope that lets us celebrate Easter all year long."

But Edmund couldn't continue. His cough got louder and louder. His mom and dad helped him back into bed.

Ebenezer turned to Hope and asked, "Just how sick is he?"

"Very sick, I'm afraid."

Hope touched Ebenezer's coat,
and he found himself back in
St. Bart's Church. He gazed up at
the beautiful stained-glass
windows—each one a different
picture, as Hope began to sing:

There's a story that started on Christmas,

When a baby was born in the night.

And those who came far—who followed the star

Were seeing a heavenly sight.

The years hurried by, and the boy, now a man,

Could make the blind see with the touch of his hand.

He was born to be King—he was Rabbi and Priest.

But the best that he had, he gave to the least.

He was born and he died—almost 2000 years ago.

He laughed and he cried—he felt all the fears we know.

He hated injustice—he taught what is right.

He said, "I'm the Way and the Truth and the Light."

His friends soon believed that he was the one,
The Savior, Messiah; in fact, God's own Son.
But others, they doubted, they did not agree.
So they took him, they tried him; he died on a tree.

"That's how it ends?" Ebenezer asked.

"No, Ebenezer," Hope replied, and pointed to the very last window.

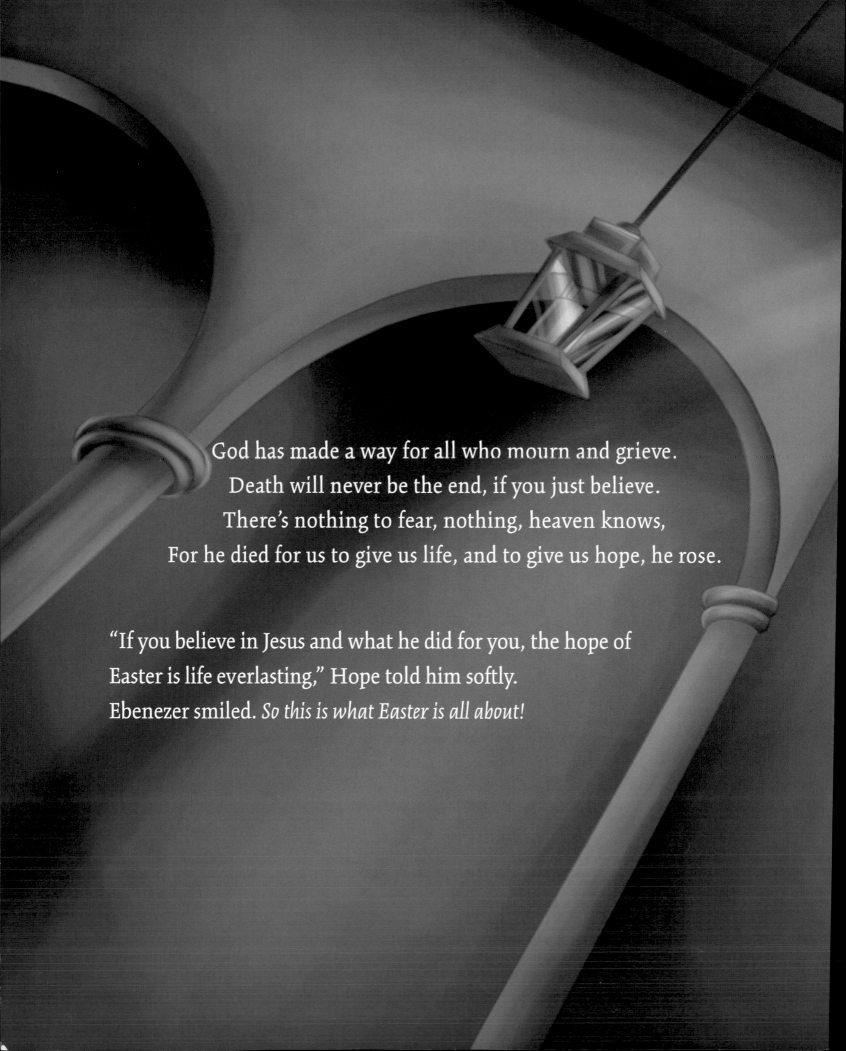

God has made a way for all who mourn and grieve.
Death will never be the end, if you just believe.
There's nothing to fear, nothing, heaven knows,
For he died for us to give us life, and to give us hope, he rose.

"If you believe in Jesus and what he did for you, the hope of
Easter is life everlasting," Hope told him softly.
Ebenezer smiled. *So this is what Easter is all about!*

Hope looked down sadly. "Of course, some people wish this church had never been here."

CRASH!

Ebenezer jumped as a huge wrecking ball smashed through the first window. Colored glass burst into thousands of tiny pieces.

"Welcome to Easter Future," Hope shouted, as they ran into the street.

Ebenezer looked down the street and saw a little girl selling pencils. Hope explained that the girl had no home. She had once lived in the church orphanage, supported by people filled with the hope of Easter. But now that the church was gone, so was the orphanage.

Then Ebenezer watched as a thief snuck up and stole her tin cup.

"Stop!" yelled a police officer. But he didn't run after the thief.

He was too afraid.

The angel explained, "Without the hope of Easter, no one is willing to risk his life for someone else."

Then Hope turned Ebenezer around to see Reverend Gilbert walk away from a tombstone in the cemetery. The stone read "Edmund Gilbert."

"Hope! What have I done?" Ebenezer shouted. "It can't end this way. We have to change the future! Hope? We need you!"

But the music box had wound down.
Only the egg remained.
  "Oh no!" Ebenezer yelled, running as
fast as he could to St. Bart's Church.

CRASH!

The wrecking ball smashed through the church.

"Stop!" Ebenezer yelled as the second crash destroyed the steeple. But it was too late. And now, the steeple was falling—right toward *him*.

At that moment, Ebenezer sat up and blinked. He had been sleeping. He was still on the couch in his office. Ebenezer ran to the window and spotted a little girl selling Easter lilies.

"Happy Easter, sir!" she shouted.

Easter. It wasn't too late! Ebenezer tossed her a bag of money and turned to look at his grandmother's picture hanging on the wall.

"Happy Easter, Grandmother!" he said as he dashed out of his office to save the church.

Ebenezer hurried past the frantic
mechanical chickens producing more and
more eggs. He rushed out of the factory
and through the gates.

"Now's our chance!" Cavis said.

"Maybe not," Millward answered, as
they turned to see smoke pouring out of
the factory windows.

Reverend Gilbert finished giving his Easter
message as two workmen stomped into the church.

"It's time for the church to be torn down."

Everyone watched sadly as hammers were raised and the wrecking ball was
positioned to strike.

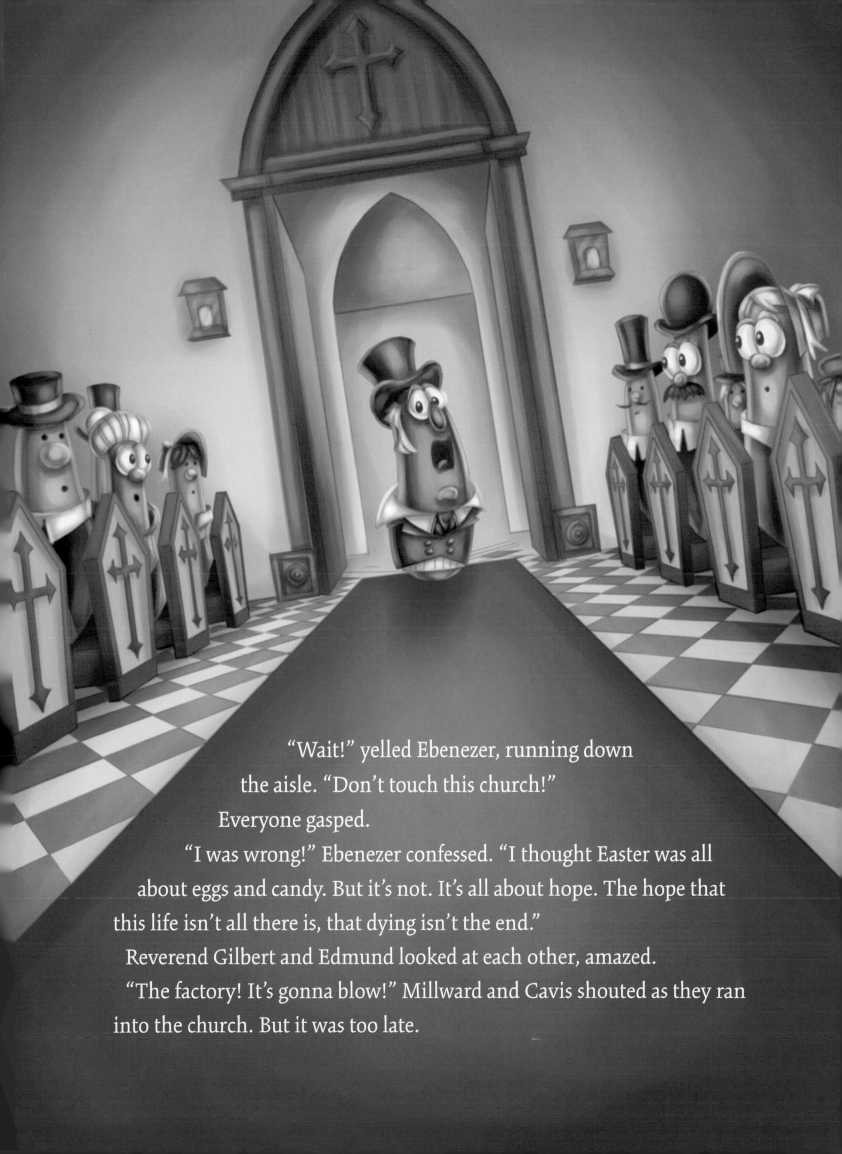

"Wait!" yelled Ebenezer, running down the aisle. "Don't touch this church!"

Everyone gasped.

"I was wrong!" Ebenezer confessed. "I thought Easter was all about eggs and candy. But it's not. It's all about hope. The hope that this life isn't all there is, that dying isn't the end."

Reverend Gilbert and Edmund looked at each other, amazed.

"The factory! It's gonna blow!" Millward and Cavis shouted as they ran into the church. But it was too late.

BOOM!

A loud explosion was heard as colorful plastic Easter eggs filled the air.

"Looks like the eggs are free this year!" Ebenezer said with a smile.

"What are you gonna do now, Mr. Nezzer?" Edmund asked as everyone
gathered around.

"I'll do what matters most! Whatever money I have left, I'll use to fix up the orphanage. Then I'll make sure *you* get your medicine," Ebenezer said with a smile.

"Easter is all about a new beginning—if you believe. *That's* what my grandmother tried to teach me."

There is nothing left to fear,
Nothing, heaven knows.
For he died for us to give us life,
And to give us hope, he rose.